They're fANTastic!

Usborne Bug Tales

The Really Evil Weevil

Russell Punter

Illustrated by Siân Roberts

This story's all about a bug who tries hard to be evil...

You'll meet Stan Snail,

Beth Bee,

Fred Flea

 and teeny Steve the weevil.

Here is Steve the weevil.

He's very, very small.

The other bugs don't notice him.

"They don't know who I am."

"If I'm an **evil** weevil...

they'll do just what I say."

10

"I'll work out lots of tricks and traps."

He plots the night away.

11

The next day,
Steve is ready.

"My first plan's
sure to scare."

12

"Once Stan Snail slithers on my plank, I'll shoot him through the air!"

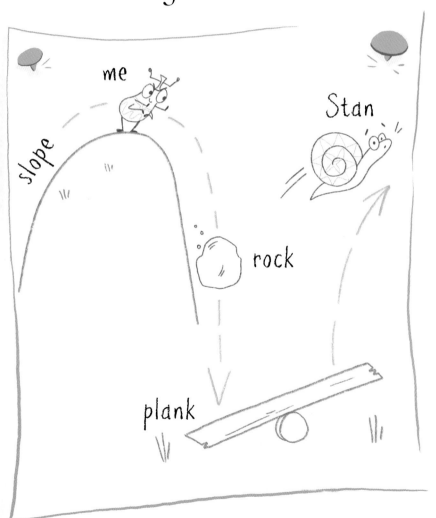

He finds a very
heavy rock...

...and shoves
it up the slope.

Stan the snail comes
gliding by.

Whew!
Nearly at
the top...

But then the rock
starts rolling back...

...and Steve can't
make it stop.

THUD! Poor Steve gets flattened.

Things haven't gone to plan.

He's feeling dazed
and shaken.

"Are you okay?" asks Stan.

19

Steve limps back to his drawing board.

"A pile of ice in
Beth Bee's house...

...will leave her
freezing cold."

Steve flies high,
above Beth's house.

But as he tries to drop
the cubes...

...they all begin to stick.

"I'm f...frozen to the ice," wails Steve.

Beth buzzes out to
see what's wrong.

Hi Steve!
You do
look blue.

Steve flies home. He thaws and thinks. "How tricky can this be?"

I'll show Fred Flea I'm really mean!

"I'll drop dung from a tree!"

He sets his trap and
waits for Fred.

Steve shoves the dung...

...but it stays put.

"Perhaps the dung is stuck?" thinks Steve.

It lands **splat** on his head.

Fred runs back. He heard Steve's cry.

Eww! What's been going on?

Steve's had enough of
evil schemes.

Steve has a bath.
He's feeling sad.

Then comes a knock
upon his door...

"We heard that you got squashed...

...and cold...

...and something made you smell."

"So we've popped by
to say hello

and make sure
that you're well."

"I didn't know you cared,"
says Steve.

"Of course," the others say.

Now Steve feels bad
about his tricks.

That night, he draws up
three new plans.

They're ready the next day.

The first's a slide-in
Snail Wash.

Next comes
a honey maker.

Beth can't believe her eyes.

"Oh, thank you, Steve," she cries.

He makes a trampoline
for Fred.

You'll jump
three times
as high!

Fred loves bouncing
up and down.

I think **I'd** like
to try.

You don't need to be evil
to let bugs know you're there.

Being kind is nicer
and you'll find out soon...

...they care!

Designed by Laura Nelson Norris
Edited by Lesley Sims
Reading consultant: Alison Kelly

First published in 2024 by Usborne Publishing Limited, 83-85 Saffron Hill, London EC1N 8RT, United Kingdom. usborne.com Copyright © 2024 Usborne Publishing Limited. The name Usborne and the Balloon logo are registered trade marks of Usborne Publishing Limited. All rights reserved. No part of this publication may be reproduced, stored in a retrieval system or transmitted in any form or by any means without prior permission of the publisher. UE.